MW00899974

The Bat That Came To Breakfast

STORY BY
H.D. VESSER

ILLUSTRATED BY
ANA RANKOVIC

For Joe my love and partner in life who believed in me and financed this project and the series.

For Whitney (who always loves a good story)

For Jennie who saved me (literally) from the horror of my home life when I was a teenager.

For Pauline, who I know looks down on me from her place in heaven (I will love her forever.)

For Elaine...my greatest Bart The Bat fan.

For anyone in life who encouraged me to be creative instead of putting me in a box as I was growing up.

To creativity! Where would I be without you?

And to "Bartworld." Any time I feel overwhelmed by the world I can go there and work on another book for the series. (it makes me feel that the world can be a better place) It always makes me release a big sigh of relief.

THAT world feels safe. I love it so!

© Copyright 2018 H. D. Vesser

To :

Joe, Whitney, Jennie, Pauline, Elaine,
anyone who encouraged me in life to be creative.

And of course...the bat who came to breakfast.

H.D. Vesser

Once upon a time, when animals could talk and girls were brave, and moms were——well, annoying, (but well loved) there was a little girl named Zoe who liked bats.

She wanted to sleep like a bat.

She liked to eat like a bat.

She LOVED to act like a bat.

But when she was in school no one wanted her to hang upside down at her desk.

Or scream "Topor!!!!" (which is the bat word for hibernation) in her best vampire-ish voice every time she was asked to do a math problem.

She had dreams in bat... flying wildly, chasing bugs in her dreams.

She even asked her mother if she could have one for a pet.

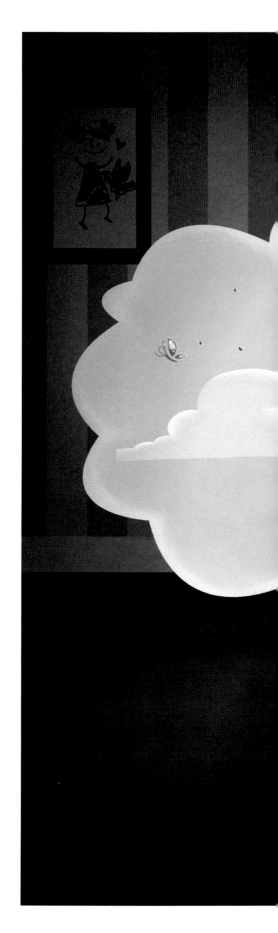

But the bats must have heard her, because one day... a bat came to breakfast!

"Guano!" screamed the bat!

"AHHHHH!" Zoe's mother screamed!

But Zoe knew bat talk, so she thought she would educate her mother.

She turned to tell her mother what guano meant.

"Ew" said mom. "It's bat poop?"

Zoe's mother ran to the closet for a broom.

Her mother said "What are you doing inviting a bat to breakfast?"

"Actually Mommy, I think he needs to use the bathroom."

"What?" she asked.

"I told you...guano means bat droppings!"

"I'm afraid we can't have him using up the toilet paper," said her mother, who was on the phone with the police. "You have to help me get this bat out of my house!" she screamed hysterically.

The bat stared, worried, at Zoe's mother. The bat didn't like that at all.

He tried to change the subject.

"Do you know in China my name is Foo?"
"Which kind of rhymes with... Bartholomew!"
"Bats are all lucky in China."

He spread his wings upside down on the fireplace with a big yawn.

Which scared her mom again.

This wasn't going very well.

"My name is Bartholomew——or Bart for short. Bart the bat, at your service!" The bat said, dodging a steely eyed glare from Zoe's mother as she swung at him with her broom.

"You really do talk!" exclaimed Zoe.

"So what's your name?" asked Bart.

Since the bat had such a cool name, Zoe had to throw in her favorite thing in the world to do.

Zoe loved to sing.

"My name is Zoe. Zoe the zinger!!" and she proceeded to ziiiing, flinging her arms in the air!

"I'm Zart the Zat!" Said Bart, stretching out his wings and letting out a note, but he landed on his head on the fireplace ledge.

"Ouch! How did you do that?" asked Bart.

Zoe didn't know what to say to that.

But she could see it was hard for a bat, (who was used to flying) to zing upside down.

She returned to her cereal and said to the bat "you want some breakfast?"

"Zoe we don't want him eating all the pancakes!" said Zoe's mother, wagging her finger in front of the bat. "He'll get his slimy little claws all over my nice clean table." she said, approaching with the broom and garbage can shield.

She talked excitedly on the phone, now to the fire station.

Then they transferred her to ANOTHER phone number. She had been on the phone for an hour.

"No one is helping me get rid of that bat!" she growled.

Zoe turned to her mom. "But bats don't eat pancakes! They eat bugs! I'm going to go catch some!"

"Nooooooo!" Said Zoe's mother... "YOU NEED TO GET HIM OUT OF HERE—NOW!"

"No!" said Zoe.

"Here!" interrupted Bart, jumping off the fireplace ledge and landing in a perfect bat crouch. "I'll help you fnd some nice juicy BUGS!"

"Close your eyes, grab my hand—I mean wing!" said the bat.

Zoe grabbed onto Bart's wing.

Right as he flew into the sliding glass door.

Thunk!

"Oh!" said Bart. "It's bright out there!"

Zoe's mom opened the sliding glass door.

Zoe was now hanging of her mom's leg.

She tried to help her new friend get away, but her mother waved her broom at Bart.

"GET OUT!"

"Mom, you just don't understand. He's all alone—oh no!"

With a backward glance Bart the bat flew out the door.

Leaving Zoe behind in his haste to get outside away from the angry, broom- swinging woman who was Zoe's mom.

"MOM!" yelled Zoe dejectedly.

"I'm just glad he's gone." said her mother.

"I'm not." said Zoe under her breath. "This is what I always wanted, and you ruined it!"

Zoe went to her room and cried.

Later that night, Zoe was sitting alone sad on her bed when she heard a noise.

She looked everywhere, hugging her stuffed bat.

Then she heard it again. She thought it was coming from the window.

She opened the curtains to see Bart clinging to the window. He looked terrified. His big bat wings stretched out across the window hanging on for dear life.

"HELP!!!" said Bart.

"You want to come back in?" asked Zoe.

"Well, I don't know... you sure scared my mom." said Zoe as she opened the window to help him in.

They sat down in front of her bed. Bart sighed.

"Well at night I sleep in a cave." said Bart.

"I'm lost and I don't know where it is."

"I'm scared." whispered Bart, his eyes darting around in fear.

"Can't you use your senses to find your way?" asked Zoe.

"I can use my senses to see where bugs are, but I can't find my cave. I seem to have lost it." said Bart.

"Well... I have a big gingerbread house on my dresser," said Zoe.

"You can stay there if you want," said Zoe excitedly.

"Maybe for a while this can be our secret!" exclaimed Zoe, looking around to make sure her mother wasn't near.

Bart yawned and sleepily crawled into the gingerbread house.

And that is how Bart the bat came to stay at Zoe's house.

Shhhhhhhhhhh...

END

Thanks a million to Ana (my illustrator) who seems to understand my crazy explanations of what I want for the series and this book.

Thank you to FinalStraw (who allowed me to use their design and straw for the book) "Suck responsibly" (I DO!) https://finalstraw.com/ Check out their mermaid commercial on the website... it's BRILLIANT! (I think I have watched it a million times, it makes me laugh so hard!)

Thank you to Adam J. Foster for helping me illustrate my first version concept of Bart.

And a special thank you to the BAT that showed up at my house (I had to get him out of my house as no service would help me in my area!) There would be no book without him~ He inspired these books!
H.D. Vesser

Thank you to Igor who supported Ana while she was working on this book... and doing all the dishes.
A. Rankovic

"For more of Bart's adventures and to keep informed on the latest books, Bart's latest thoughts, and where you can meet Bart's new friends visit
www.bartthebat.com."

H.D. Vesser lives in Washington State where they love looking out the window at their desk watching the hummingbirds, birds, and nature writing about Bart. (Watch for the series!)

A. Rankovic, illustrator from Belgrade Serbia
does what she loves most... draws cartoony characters :)

All rights reserved. This book and it's illustrations are protected by copyright. You may not adapt, modify, publish, distribute, or reproduce (for fees or otherwise) in any media or form or by any means, the whole or any part of this book or it's illustrations to any person or organization without the prior written consent of H. D. Vesser, the copyright owner. Where provided to you in electronic format, you may only print one copy for your personal non-commercial use. Failure to comply with the terms of this warning may expose you to legal action for copyright infringement.

59909574R00024

Made in the USA
Columbia, SC
09 June 2019